WHEN GOD
GAVE US WORDS

SANDY EISENBERG SASSO is the Director of Religion, Spirituality and the Arts Initiative at Indiana University–Purdue University at Indianapolis (IUPUI) Arts and Humanities Institute. She is also Rabbi Emerita of Congregation Beth-El Zedeck and the author of *Midrash: Reading the Bible with Question Marks* and award-winning children's books, including *God's Paintbrush* and *In God's Name*. She is the coauthor of *Who Counts? 100 Sheep, 10 Coins, and 2 Sons* and *The Marvelous Mustard Seed*. Both titles were Junior Library Guild selections.

DARCY DAY ZOELLS loves telling stories with pictures, but she also loves words! She found that imagining the world before language was a wonderful creative journey. She is a graduate of Northwestern University and a member of the Society of Children's Book Writers and Illustrators. She lives with her family outside of Chicago. You can see more of Darcy's work at www.darcydayzoells.com.

• • •

Text © 2018 Sandy Eisenberg Sasso
Illustrations © 2018 Darcy Day Zoells

First edition
Published by Flyaway Books
Louisville, Kentucky

18 19 20 21 22 23 24 25 26 27—10 9 8 7 6 5 4 3 2 1

Book design by Allison Taylor
Illustrations created by Darcy Day Zoells with watercolor and ink on Arches cold press paper and digitally collaged.

Library of Congress Cataloging-in-Publication Data
Names: Sasso, Sandy Eisenberg, author. | Zoells, Darcy Day, illustrator.
Title: The words God gave us / Sandy Eisenberg Sasso ; Darcy Day Zoells, illustrator.
Description: Louisville, Kentucky : Flyaway Books, 2018. | Summary: Over the protests of the angels, God gives people words but quickly reconsiders as lies, curses, and gossip appear but soon, words are being used in new, beautiful ways.
Identifiers: LCCN 2018007804 | ISBN 9781947888012 (hardback)
Subjects: | CYAC: Language and languages--Fiction. | Vocabulary--Fiction. | God--Fiction. | Angels--Fiction. | Creation--Fiction. | BISAC: JUVENILE FICTION / Legends, Myths, Fables / General. | JUVENILE FICTION / Religious / Christian / General.
Classification: LCC PZ7.S24914 Wor 2018 | DDC [E]--dc23 LC record available at https://lccn.loc.gov/2018007804

PRINTED IN CHINA

Most Flyaway Books are available at special quantity discounts when purchased in bulk by corporations, organizations, and special-interest groups. For more information, please e-mail SpecialSales@flyawaybooks.com.

Sandy Eisenberg Sasso

WHEN GOD GAVE US WORDS

Illustrated by Darcy Day Zoells

flyaway
books

Louisville, Kentucky

One day God decided to give words to man and woman.

But the angels objected.

"People will not know what to do with words.
Words should belong only to angels."

But God said, "Perhaps people will make something beautiful with words."

"Nothing could be more wonderful than what we do with words," the angels insisted. "People will just mess them up."

But God was intent on hearing words
from the mouths of men and women.
So God filled the angels' sacks with words
and sent the angels to earth
to spread the words.

In some sacks God put long, difficult words like "omniscient" and "antidisestablishmentarianism."

The angels frowned. "People will never understand the meaning of these words."

And it was so. Because of the long, difficult words, dictionaries were created.

In other sacks, God put silly words like "gibberish," "goop," and "gosh."

In one sack, God placed all the words that were hard to spell, like "hors d'oeuvres."

"People will never know how to spell those words," said the angels.

And it was so. Because of hard-to-spell words, God created spelling lists.

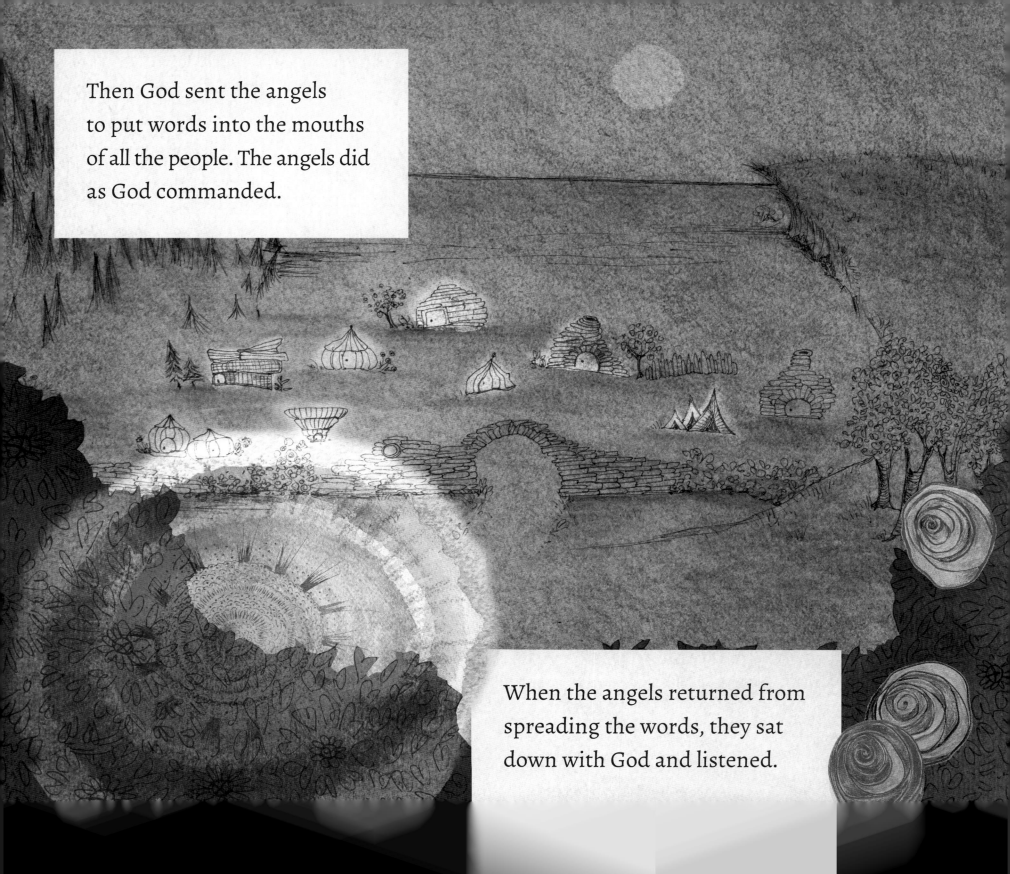

Then God sent the angels
to put words into the mouths
of all the people. The angels did
as God commanded.

When the angels returned from
spreading the words, they sat
down with God and listened.

It took some time for people to get accustomed to using words. Slowly they let each word form in their mouths. Carefully, they added one to another to another until they made sentences.

When they got used to the words,
they talked and talked and talked
until the angels shouted,

ENOUGH!

But God wanted to hear more.

Then people twisted and turned words
and made lies.

They rolled words in the wet earth
until they were covered with mud
and created curses.

People mixed words
with sharp thorns,
and gossip was born.

The angels shouted,
"Stop! What a mess
people are making
with our words."

And God regretted giving words to man and woman.

God was about to send the angels
to earth, to take back all the words,
when God heard a new sound.

People stirred soft music into words
and sang lullabies.

Words were mixed with dance,
and poetry was born.

People joined laughter
to words and told jokes.

The angels smiled and
said to God, "Some of
these jokes are very funny,
and some are just silly."

And it was so. For the silly jokes, God created groans, and for the truly funny jokes, God just laughed!

People mixed words with midnight and wrote mysteries. When the angels listened to the mysteries, their wings trembled.

People wove longing, thanksgiving, and hope into words and offered prayer.

Imagination and words were joined together,
and then there were stories.

The angels listened and were enchanted.

God asked the angels if they still wanted to gather all the words and bring them back to the heavens.

The angels remembered the lies and the curses and the gossip that people had made with words.

Nevertheless, the angels did not want to take back the words.

They loved the songs and poetry
that people had created. They giggled
at the jokes and cried during prayers.

"We must hear the end of the stories the people are telling," the angels pleaded.

And it was so. People were allowed to keep the gift of words,

for the sake of stories.